The Cold Planet

The Cold Planet

Sooner or later, everything comes to an end! The greatest fears of mankind have been realized. The Sun, the star that shone so brightly for many years and warmed the entire planet Earth with its warmth, gradually lost its abilities. The Sun began to fade away, and with it, life on the planet began to fade away. People were dying from the cold, but some higher power, watching over all of humanity, gave it a second chance A chance for a new life, when it seemed that it would be impossible to give birth, a child is born. A new generation of superhumans who have a chance to survive on a cold planet... But not everyone was happy about this news, because ordinary people also wanted to avoid the cold and so they started hunting ....

But how will it end?

ISBN: 9798342898911

Ruslana Okhrimenko

The Cold Planet

1

Everything comes to an end eventually! Any product can expire, so don't the planet's resources belong to this category? Moreover, the resources of the universe, which is already limitless and completely immense, can also come to its historical end at some point. And so it happened!

To avoid scaring people with the future, I won't mention the year, as the apprehensions of mankind regarding the immense star known as the Sun have been proven to be justified. The temperature of the Sun has dropped, not much at first, but over the years it has started to go down more and more!

However, humans are cunning creatures! They have an incredible gift for adapting to everything. This time, they have succeeded, again. Because life on the planet has hardly changed, except for the low temperature. Even people began to get used to the cold weather over time. Of course, a lot of materials were consumed to keep warm. It was hard for those, who lived on warm continents, as some people simply could not stand the unaccustomed temperature difference and died. However, it was not easy for the people of the north, although it is rarely +15 degrees Celsius there, just very rare! But even for them, such a sharp deterioration in the weather was difficult.

People and the authorities tried to pretend that everything was under control, that everything was normal, but everyone felt the changes. The cold snap had a negative impact on the elderly, they became more sick and the mortality rate of people over 60 years doubled. The birth rate has decreased! Because pregnant women were often exposed to freezing temperatures, their babies were very weak, so most of them were born sick or even dead. Because of this, the world lost more than two million babies and even more pensioners.

Life on the planet seemed impossible, but humans are still cunning creatures who seem to be loved by God very much, because the first baby was born. After five years of childlessness. This sensation was broadcast on all the TV channels, printed in all the newspapers, and the Internet was buzzing about this baby. It was a boy, completely healthy, he was breathing, behaving as a baby should. But there was one thing: he was cold! No thermometer showed his body temperature, his skin felt like a cold corpse, but he was not dead. His organs were not working as they should, but slower. His heart was beating two beats slower than a normal person's heart. And because of this, the blood was not as thin as usual, and its color was darker red, almost black. It was because of the black-looking blood that such people were called "Inkwellers". It is difficult to understand why this name was chosen, but it became as old as a leech. Scientists decided to give these individuals a different, more scientific name. Therefore, they were listed in the documents as "HomoSuperior", like a new unique species of human. Children of the future!

At first, these children were considered an anomaly because they were born very rarely, but then the population of "Inkwellers" became larger than the population of ordinary people. Even in the schools where the children studied, there was a kind of racism against dark-blooded children. They were openly hated by both, children and adults! Both on the same level. Adults could beat children with dark blood, and for some reason this behavior was not punished in the modern world. But such people were more disliked because of their abilities. Because these humans did not freeze on the coldest nights, they moved very quickly, almost as if they were vampires, and they could jump as high as five stories. Their mental abilities are exceptionally high. They were like real vampires who were not afraid of daylight (although it was quite gloomy). Scientists were seriously puzzled by this phenomenon. They studied and examined newborn babies who had this feature. Some scientists became increasingly desperate and demanded permission to conduct experiments because they wanted to use the unique blood to develop a vaccine. One scientist thought of dissecting his own daughter to understand how the organs of such special children work. He believed that they had a different structure of the insides. But he was stopped in time. Because of all this, a hunt was launched for the " Inkwellers". Within ten years, the scientists managed to obtain the permit, as temperatures dropped even further, and only individuals with dark blood could survive the severe cold. So, they started hiding!

There were guards on the streets, who checked the temperature of all passers-by, and if it was insanely low, the person was detained for no reason. Parents became afraid for their children and were forced to hide them in their homes or take them to villages far from the checkpoints.

However, not all parents were so caring, because some consented to have their children used in experiments at birth. These are really horrible and terrible people, or rather non-humans. Personally, I don't understand how you can give your own child, your own blood, as an unnecessary thing to those beasts. Death is better! Life was becoming increasingly difficult, and this parody of life turned into real survival. The strongest survived, and we were part of this society.

The Cold Planet

2

There are four of us and we live under one small roof that barely protects us from the rain. Although, it is a small room in an abandoned hut on the outskirts of the city, everyone has their own corner. We built bunk beds and it looked like the room had two floors. On the top floor, I sleep on a soft mattress with my little brother Vilas, because there is no guarantee that the structure, we built is strong, and because he and I are the lightest in our group. If we fall, no one will get hurt badly. Our snorers, Markus and Rad, are sleeping below. They are older than me, but not by much - Marcus is three years older and Rad is four years older. And I am Viola, and I am 16.

Of course, we are not all blood relatives, we were not born by the same mother and we were not brought up in the same family, but most likely it is the family, or rather the lack of it, that is the problem. It's not that our parents abandoned us; on the contrary, they defended us until the end, and because they wanted to protect our rights, they were killed. An incredibly horrible death. I still miss them to this day. I know that even in his silence, Vilas cries at night, longing for our happy past.

We are all united by a common problem, the solution to which we cannot find. But we are still alive, and so we can enjoy certain little things in life. No matter how hard it may be sometimes.

Rad and Markus work underground jobs, or rather part-time jobs. This month they changed about thirty jobs each. It's a big number, but they could take something useful from each job, albeit clandestinely. Rad from his job in a store stole for us vegetables and many other food items, which lasted us almost a month. Marius from the mattress store where he used to work, when he was running away, took a couple of rolled up light mattresses with him. He was found out, so he could not stay there for long. Of course, there was no chase after him because he was lucky. Marius was exposed by a colleague at work, she accidentally touched him and realized everything. So, without saying anything and without waiting for the guards, Marius ran away. Instead of his salary, he took out mattresses for us. He grabbed the first ones he could find. They were small, but mature. He said that passersby looked at him very strangely when they saw him with these big things. I'm not sure if I've said it before, but if I have, I'd like to remind you that dark-blooded people are physically stronger than ordinary people and more resilient. That is why it was not difficult for Marcus to carry those mattresses. However, I am certain that it would be difficult for ordinary people.

The Cold Planet

There have been many similar situations, but the primary challenge lies in the search process. It's a pointless hunt for animals, just because people are afraid of us and in a sense want to tame us. No one would mind if they found a vaccine that would save people from the cold, but not at such a terrible cost. More people died from such experiments than during the Holodomor in general, and there were several of them. I read this in a book that Marcus took with him when he fled the bookstore where he was also exposed. However, there was a more piquant story there, and on the one hand it was funny. He is a good-looking guy, and therefore could be popular with girls and not only (under different circumstances, of course). There was also a woman working in the bookstore. A lonely widow, in short! And she read novels about heroes in love with a bottle of wine and courted visitors. Sometimes she was lucky, and sometimes she was not. When she was alone with Marcus when the store was empty, she began to show him unwanted attention and pinned him in one corner of the bookshelves. There she found out the truth he was hiding by kissing him on the lips.

We laughed about this situation for a long time, because this is how Marcus had his first kiss. He had never been so close to anyone in a physical way. However, the most interesting thing was her reaction. She shouted after the running away guy whose secret was exposed: "I will accept you as you are, just be with me!" Our stomachs were bursting with laughter, while Marcus' cheeks were burning with shame.

Of course, the «Inkwellers» have found a way to adapt even in crowded cities, and some of them, I think, may even be in power. Because it's cold, most people wear gloves, and we do too. We try to avoid walking or running fast, and most importantly, we try not to touch others. The worst part was to came to the hospital, because to get to the hospital is the end of the line! Everyone is acutely aware of the hopelessness of the situation, and I am sure that many of the dark-blooded individuals would agree to donate blood, but they would definitely not agree to die. Because everyone wants to live; this is evident without needing any confirmation.

The Cold Planet

3

Tonight's dinner was organized by Marcus. He managed to get two large and flavorful pizzas with ham and a lot of fragrant cheese.

"Mmm, where did you get them, Marcus?" Vilas asked, shoving one piece into his mouth. His curls tumbled playfully across his forehead. He reminded me of my father, even though he was only twelve.

"A good friend of mine from Todd's pizzeria where I used to work," Marcus replied happily. His pointy nose moved funny when he spoke, but his voice was pleasant to listen to. He had a pleasant timbre.

"Oh, the cook?" I asked again, grabbing the hot piece of pizza with cold hands. Although, to ordinary people, it would definitely seem cold.

"Yes, Lurie - he was able to repay me in this way because I helped him unload the car with food today," Marcus rested his hands by his sides, content in the knowledge that his family was well-fed. "You did well!" I praised him, eating one triangle with a large piece of ham.

"Yes, but unfortunately, that's all for today," Marcus said sadly without even touching the pizza.

"Vilas, don't eat all of it! Leave some for Rad!" I slapped his hand, which was reaching for the fourth piece.

"By the way, where is he?" Marcus asked, looking at me with his brown eyes.

"He's working," I answered hesitantly, because Rad had asked me not to tell him anything, but Vilas had never been able to keep a secret, so he blurted it out.

"In a diner? Downtown?! Is he crazy?"

Marcus was not happy to hear this. The center is the most dangerous place for us. But there are a lot of dark-blooded people working there, because that's the kind of person who helped him to get employed. He seems normal, but Marcus' paranoia turned a good man into a criminal:

"Don't you seriously understand? He could be a fake, sent on purpose to find us and turn us in to the authorities!" Marcus began to gather his things at a frantic pace.

"Where are you going?" Vilas asked in alarm, his eyes bulging.

"For Rad! I'll get him out of there!" he was putting on his jacket.

"And if you get caught? I'm sure Rad will handle it!" I tried to stop him.

Rad was even faster than Marcus. He always tried not to stand out. He was tall, slender, but rather thin, often hunching over, and never losing his optimism.

"Yeah, of course he is! He's a year older than me, but he's got less brains than Vilas!" Marcus was furious.

"Hey, that was insulting," Vilas furrowed his brow. He hadn't expected such rudeness.

We all knew it wasn't true.

"Really, dude! You can take offense to that, and that's what I want to do right now," Rad's tired voice called back. He was standing in the doorway with a bag full of goodies, as we first thought. "Watch what you say, because sometimes your words can hurt," Rad reprimanded Marcus, and smiled at the corners of his lips.

"Okay," Marcus rolled his eyes. "I was just worried."

And for good reason. Because once there were five of us. But no one talks about Dana as if she never existed. It's a taboo to mention her.

DANA

Of course, I have to mention her because she is part of our history, and history is always worth remembering. It teaches us! History shows us how certain events or decisions affected society and allows us to avoid repeating mistakes. For example, studying military conflicts or economic crises helps to understand their causes and consequences, which can help prevent similar situations in the future. However, sometimes it seems that history teaches us nothing, or people just like to keep making the same mistakes.

Many contemporary events have deep roots in historical processes. Understanding what happened before helps to better interpret current events, political or social changes. The memory of historical tragedies helps to shape moral principles and contributes to the development of a more ethical society. I think this is exactly what we will become when all this genocide against our species is over.

Vilas and I, joined this group when there were three of them - Rad, Dana and Marcus! Their parents were friends and together they resisted the guards and the authorities who wanted to take the children for experiments. When their parents were killed, the three were left alone with their problems. As teenagers, it was difficult to exist in a world where you were persecuted at every turn.

Dana was an activist! She tried to organize rallies in defense of dark-blooded people, despite not being one herself. Thanks to this, they managed to hold out longer. Dana was the one, who found places and shelters where they could stay safely.

I didn't spend much time with her personally, but within a year, it became clear that she and Marcus had developed feelings for each other. It's really hard to resist his charm and appearance. I didn't realize it at first, but as I got older, I also started to notice these traits of a man. He is caring, takes responsibility for his life and not only. You can trust him, he keeps his word, and he is attentive to details. I'm sure that's what Dana liked about him. Although, it is also possible that he was a dark-blooded creature of the planet. She was on our side and that was important.

Back then, we lived in another place where we each had our own room. Dana called it a dormitory, but no students had lived there for a long time. It was an old abandoned building with wind blowing in from everywhere. Broken windows on the upper floors, a space that stands silently under the weight of time, full of memories, but no longer breathing fresh life. The facade of the building has been eaten away by years of bad weather: faded, peeling, with cracks running along the walls like thin scars. In some places, the paint, which was once bright, has peeled off, revealing gray and dull bricks. The concrete staircase is crumbling in some places. The air is thick and musty, tinged with moisture and dust. Every corner is full of quiet rustling, as if the memory of those who once lived here still lives on. On the walls, you can sometimes see old graffiti or notes from students who dreamed of the future, not knowing that these dreams have long since dissipated. There were such strange inscriptions in my room. I could only make out a few names, but everything else was erased over time.

The best thing about this place was that no one was looking for us here. This dormitory had been searched a long time ago and nothing was found, so they forgot about it. And it was to our advantage.

It was within these walls that something more than just love between two young people was born. A new life was born here. In the past, this age would not have been considered sufficient to become parents, but now no one cared if a seventeen-year-old teenager became pregnant. However, the government would take an interest if that pregnant teenager turned out to be one of the "Inkwellers". Of course, Dana was an ordinary person with warm blood, but Marcus...

We found out about Dana's pregnancy as unexpectedly as she did. At first, she started to worry that she didn't have regular menstruation (I never found out what it was, apparently, it's a feature of normal women). However, she did not panic, because her cycle often changed due to temperature changes and even had a break of several months. Dana said that it had never happened before.

We started to worry a lot, when she vomited farther than she could see (literally). The girl simply could not eat, because she was sick from everything. That's when we took a desperate step and went to the hospital. In general, she is an ordinary person, so Dana was received with a smile. The most frightening moment for her was filling out the paperwork, as she was afraid that the information that her parents were insurgents would come out. But her excitement was too much, because I don't think they can bring up this kind of archival data in the hospital.

And my opinion was right, because nothing happened and Dana was admitted. As she told me, they took her blood for tests (I had never been through such a procedure). Although it may seem strange, she urinated into a jar, and after receiving the test results, the doctor informed her of her pregnancy.

With this information, Dana returned to us. Marcus was in a state of anticipation. He walked around the room with wide strides, so loud that the whole building vibrated. When she came to us, I still remember her face. She was upset and confused! Her eyes were running from side to side and it seemed like tears were about to come, but she was not the type to cry. So, she answered many of Marcus' questions in a calm voice shortly:

"I'm pregnant!"

Her eyes searched for something in Marcus's face. Some kind of response, but he was cold in his feelings. I'm sure that many questions were going through his mind at that moment, but he didn't dare to voice them. The only thing he could do was ask a question:

"What are we going to do?"

What to do? To live! Continue to fight for what we have been fighting for. And to do it more! I was honestly happy for Dana and supported her in everything, even though I was still too young to be an aunt. Together we came up with names for different genders of children. It was clear that our tastes did not match, and sometimes our imaginations went to the point of absurdity.

As time went on, Marcus also began to show concern for the baby in the womb. However, there was a certain tension between Dana and Marcus. I thought that such a situation should bring them closer together, but this pregnancy drove them apart. Only later did I find out what the real reason was.

After registering with the hospital, they found out that the fetus was developing well, but there was one peculiarity. The child was one of us! In general, this did not surprise me, given who the father was. But the doctors were not given this information. Dana said that she did not know who the child's father was and that the child was not wanted. It was partly true! After that, she was offered various options from which she had to choose. And she chose, revealing the whole truth.

Around the seventh month, Marcus began to pay more attention to Dana and her rounded tummy. He brought her sweets and all sorts of goodies that she wanted. Despite the poor conditions in which this young family was being raised, everything was going quite smoothly. We were still living in that old dormitory, trying to make it as comfortable as possible. The guys brought clothes for the babies, and Marcus, showing his resourcefulness, even crafted a crib out of old pieces of wood. I put soft pillows in it, and the kind people at the hospital gave Dana a big package of baby blankets and diapers. Life seemed to be going well and with the arrival of the baby, it was going to sparkle with new colors.

The worst moment was that we could not attend the birth. Marcus could not find a place for himself! He simply could not sit in the dormitory knowing that his beloved was giving birth. He wanted so much to hold the baby, to support Dana in this difficult moment. Even when asked if he would rather have a boy or a girl, he said: "It doesn't matter, as long as the baby is healthy." It sounded very sweet.

He did not respond to all the pleas and persuasions to stay at home, determined to face whatever challenges lay ahead. So, after buying some sweets, he ran to the hospital, risking being caught. He bravely approached the reception desk asking about Dana and was directed to the hospital, despite the lies. He introduced himself as her work colleague. It was there, in room 304, that he saw her. Dana was lying alone in the room! It seemed like a great luxury. When he went inside, Marcus realized that the child was not with her mother.

"Where is the baby?" he asked.

"Aren't you at all interested in how I feel?" Dana answered with a question, looking away.

'Where is the baby?" Marcus asked again.

Dana just turned her head to the other side, hiding her tears.

"I had no choice, Marcus," she said in a trembling voice.

Throwing the packages on the floor, Marcus rushed to the registration desk, which was crowded with nurses.

"Dana Mueller, she just had a baby, where is she?" Marcus aggressively slammed his hands on the tabletop and drew the women's attention.

"Dana Mueller is in room 304!" said one of the nurses.

"I'm asking about the child!" Marcus hissed through his teeth.

"And who are you, excuse me?" the nurse began to realize a little.

While others began to call somewhere and say something into the receiver, hiding.

"WHERE IS THE BABY?!" said Marcus.

His eyes filled with tears, filling them with a shimmering glitter. His palms were clenched, filled with rage.

"Please sit down, sir," the woman said patiently, pointing to a leather-upholstered bench.

"Just tell me where the child is," the man said in a pleading voice. He was desperate.

The nurse looked at him sympathetically and said:

"I can't tell you that, sir. I'm so sorry!" her hand reached out to Marcus's bent fists and touched them gently. But she recoiled in an instant, a rush of panic flooding her as she realized that she was holding one of the "Inkwellers".

She involuntarily gasped and looked at man, crying with grief, who had never had the chance to hold his own child in his arms.

Without waiting for the guards, Marcus stormed out of the hospital, wiping his face wet with tears. When we returned home, we were expecting good news, but when we heard this (after Marcus had calmed down, of course), we were devastated.

Everyone lost hope and faith that Dana would come to us. But she did appear, despite herself. She was dressed in the same clothes she had left us in, but something had definitely changed in her, and it was not the absence of a round tummy. It was something else! I felt it more than anyone else.

Rad came out to meet her! He was the first to see her through the window and went down to her. He didn't wait for her to come up on her own.

"Just go," he asked her in a calm voice.

"Go?!" she was surprised. "I have nowhere to go. This is my home.

"What did you do with the child?" Rad asked directly.

"I had to," Dana looked away from the shame.

"Tell us!" I intervened, shouting from behind the front door.

I was hiding there from who knows what, but when I realized that she wouldn't tell the Rad anything, I decided to try it.

"Vee, don't make me do this!" she asked, and I didn't understand why. But when I didn't respond, Dana continued, "The hospital offered me several options for the child. The first one was to kill her and use her for organ harvesting. The second option was to enroll her in specialized training programs designed for individuals like you. The third is to simply kill the child. The fourth option is to send the baby to a laboratory where experiments will be conducted on them.

"And where is the baby now?" I asked when I realized that there were no more options.

"I chose the second option," tears streamed down her cheeks.

"Who was it? A girl or a boy?" I continued to ask.

"A girl," Dana answered in a trembling voice. "But she will live," she said, as if justifying herself.

I had nothing to say. It's possible that if I were in her shoes, I would have acted similarly. Hard to say. Pregnant women are very emotional and therefore not always able to make the right decisions. However, at that moment she thought it would be better than letting her baby die.

"Can I see Marcus?" Dana asked, wiping her snot on her sleeve.

"I don't think it's a good idea," Rad replied rudely.

25

Here Dana's emotions changed. Anger and aggression were coming out of her.

"He didn't want this child anyway! I knew I had made the wrong choice to keep the pregnancy. I THOUGHT YOU WOULD BE HAPPY WITH ME!" she cried, catching sight of Marcus in the window. "How wrong I was..." Dana said very quietly.

I felt sorry for her. I realized that the world is much more cruel now than it used to be. And I was even afraid to be a woman in this world. Because you will still be guilty. I hugged Dana, feeling her strong heartbeat and pleasant warmth. She was crying, hugging me with her arms and constantly apologizing. No matter what happened, I was ready to let her back into my life. But unfortunately, as in most cases, the decision is made by men. And by majority vote, it was decided to split up.

"She is a human being and should live among people," Rad said, summarizing the opinion of the male side of our team.

I, in turn, remained silent, quietly wiping the tears from my eyes. Dana's reaction was remarkable; she accepted her expulsion from the herd she had been part of for many years with a sense of pride.

The Cold Planet

Rad took her backpack with some things and she left us for the big world. Alone! But I am sure that Dana will not be lonely, she will find new friends and new company. But she will always remember us. We also remember her, but we don't talk about her, so as not to stir up painful memories.

I saw her a few times in the center. A couple of times, I saw her on TV while passing by an electrical store. She is still on our side! She supports the "Inkwellers", speaks at rallies against the current government. Despite the fact that our paths diverged, we still met sometimes.

Unfortunately, I can't say the same about Markus and Dana's little girl. There was no information about these children at all. But maybe one day we will learn about them.

***

After examining the inside of the packages in detail, we found out that they contained clothes. They weren't new, but they weren't very worn either. But for us it was an incredible gift, because nowadays it is just something out of the realm of fantasy to buy clothes. It's easier to find a roasted baby on the market than cheap clothes.

"Where did you get it?" Vilas asked with eyes full of happiness.

"A secret!" Rad winked with his left eye.

"But enough of these secrets, because I won't be able to take it anymore," Marcus continued to be nervous.

"I know what you're afraid of! You're afraid that if I get caught, you'll have to look after these brawlers yourself!" Rad began to tousle Marcus's hair, who really didn't like it.

"Fool! I'm worried about you. Go eat, I brought pizza!" Marcus said angrily and fell on his bed.

Rad smiled and began to devour the rest of the pizza. He ate it so fast that it seemed like not even a minute had passed. After Rad satisfied his hunger, he had an idea.

"Guys, let's go for a run!" he shouted happily.

"Are you sure, you're okay?" I was starting to worry.

"Of course! Let's get some air. I know a place where there will be no guards. It's an abandoned neighborhood and you can safely jump over the collapsed high-rise buildings.

"I'm in!" Vilas shouted.

The boy has always loved such things, because at 12 years he is too active. And staying at home all the time is also boring. Even though I still sometimes go out for part-time work, he is just a child and isn't allowed to work, and if he gets caught... I don't even want to think about it.

We got outside. There was a fresh, frosty smell in the air, even though this summer had once been incredibly hot. Light frost covered the barely visible grass and tall bare trees. I had seen in books that they used to have green leaves, but because of the cold, they no longer grew. It was very easy to breathe and so we were able to take off. I bent as high as I could and I saw an incredibly beautiful view of lanterns shedding their light somewhere far, far away. Beauty - in a word! I could hear the boys' light murmur, which was sometimes supplemented by laughter. I will remember this moment for the rest of my life, because they mean everything to me. We ran and jumped until we reached the very place Rad described. It was really incredible! Surprisingly, such abandoned cities had their own romance. Depending on the mood, abandoned buildings could seem beautiful when bright colors were bubbling inside; mysterious when curiosity chilled the bones; terrifying when sadness brought back sad memories and thoughts; or incredibly scary when reality knocked on the door of the mind. There was something magical about these ruins, but when you remember the reason for these broken windows, you don't really want to be in this place, because it was from these windows that children and people were taken away, pulled out like cattle to the slaughterhouse.

We didn't stay there for long, only until Vilas ran out of energy and started to sleep. We decided to go home, but on the way home, the guards noticed us. It was scary! Healthy tall armed men in black uniforms were running after us and shooting us with sleeping pills! We were almost exhausted. However, we ran as high as we could, fleeing through different residential areas. We kept running and hiding because to stop meant to surrender. We could not allow that.

The Cold Planet

There were too many guards, more than ten, and so we decided to split up, although it was always a bad idea, but this time we thought it was the right thing to do. And like all teams that always split up, we made a mistake. Vilas and I managed to fool the guards and so we escaped with a calm heart. We didn't run home, because we knew we were still being followed. I don't know how to describe it, but we could feel those eyes. Although, perhaps, this paranoia was the result of a crazy chase.

We stayed there until the morning. Exhausted, hungry, scared! We sat in this ambush like puppies abandoned by their mother. In fact, that's what we were.

As soon as the first rays of sunny overcast light appeared in the sky, we decided to run again, but not as usual. We ran like ordinary people. Even early in the morning, many were already on the street heading to work, so we blended in with the crowd. After changing our clothes a little bit, we no longer looked unusual, we were just like everyone else. And that's why they couldn't find us.

Emptiness awaited us at home. Rad and Marcus had not yet returned. All we could do was wait.

The Cold Planet

4

The next day they didn't come back again. This did not scare us too much, because the boys often stayed away from home, often for several days. But inside, our hearts were clenching with bad thoughts. This would happen when they had to work, usually far away, though they never stayed for long. Never, except for this time.

They were gone for almost a week. That's when we started to openly panic. Vilas hadn't been very good at hiding his feelings before, but now he was even more nervous than usual. He was having some kind of really unhealthy hysteria:

"They'll be back, riiight now!" he pointed to the door, hoping that it would open and our guys would be standing there.

He did this more than ten times in a row, with some breaks in between. But to no avail, as no one appeared at the door for hours. Then I brewed chamomile tea and gave it to a very agitated Vilas to calm him down a bit. He drank the whole cup in one gulp, not even waiting for the tea to cool down. I was worried, that such an abrupt change in temperature, from cold to hot, would cause some changes in him. But nothing happened. He carefully put the cup on the nightstand and hugged me.

"They're not coming back, are they?" he asked very sadly, and I understood his state of mind.

"I don't want to think about it, but I think about it all the time," I answered, hugging my brother.

"What are we going to do now? How are we going to live without them?" Vilas said, barely holding back his tears.

"You can cry! It's okay," I said.

And at that moment, Vilas broke down and started crying, and I couldn't just cry. It was as if I wanted to, but I couldn't, because some part of me realized that now I had to be a support for this child, even though I was still a child myself. Now there were only two of us left, and we both realized it, but we didn't want to admit it.

"Oh, come on, don't be so sour!" I jumped up, "I'm sure they're working somewhere. What I propose is this: let's go to Marcus'sfriend and ask him. And then we'll go to Rada's work and look for them there. I think they will help us."

As I was coming up with my next plan and actively telling it, I didn't even notice the moment when tears began to roll down my face. Although, there was a smile on my face, it was not a proof of happiness, but rather a sad smile-cover. It hid my true feelings, which I had kept inside for so long. Then Vilas came to my aid. He supported me when I supported him. It was just the two of us! It was difficult to realize this.

Even earlier, the four of us once sat down and talked about how no one should ever play hooky. It meant that we should always come home. It was only allowed to go away separately for four days, and if you went away for more than that, you might not come back, or you would never come back. This is exactly what happened to the boys, because they did not return for more than five days. This was one of the rules of our family, because we did not have mobile phones because all phones are tapped and it could be very dangerous for us. It was very easy to expose the "Inkwellers" in this way. Another rule that came into effect after the previous rule was that we had to leave the house and move to another safe one. The other shelter was the village of Kuvitka, which was located near the city where we lived. Rad's ancestors used to live there a long time ago. The house and the village were both abandoned because of rumors of widespread radiation, which was believed to be especially harmful, even fatal, to dark-blooded people, making it impossible for them to stay. But Rad assured me that this was not true, that this story was spread in order to preserve at least one place where there were no guards. Maybe there will even be people like us. It's worth a try, we have no other choice anyway, because if they were interrogated or simply searched, they will find the keys to our hut. It is not difficult to do. So, having gathered everything we needed, we set off.

There was no point in running, so we walked slowly and silently. During the entire journey, which lasted for two hours, Vilas and I did not say a word. Sometimes a few words came out of our mouths, but they were not just words. It was a kind of prayer that allowed us to see our brothers off on the road ahead. We wanted it to be easier for them than we could have imagined.

When we found the house, we were easily shocked, as its condition left much to be desired. But what we have is what we have! The yard was partially without a fence, with wild thickets of thorny and fruit trees everywhere. There were winter apple trees that would soon bear small fruits (even they had gotten used to the new natural conditions of the planet). We got inside the house, and it was no better than outside. But it was still possible to settle down.

At one point, we got scared because we heard a rustling noise. Something, or someone, was sneaking inside. The first thoughts that went through our minds were: "They found us!". We stood in the corner, trembling with fear. It was difficult to move in that moment, and the fear intensified when we saw the muzzle of a rifle appear through the window. Our eyes opened wide and we could only hear each other's heartbeats.

"Come out, now!" a confident female voice sounded, to which we did not respond. "Quickly, or I will shoot!"

Without a word, we decided to come. In front of us stood a tall woman in her thirties, blonde with long hair, a hat on her head and torn mittens on her hands. She was wearing sweater and wide sweatpants. She had an angry look, but insanely kind gray eyes.

"Who are you?" she asked.

There was a pause! We didn't know what to say, it was hard to trust an unfamiliar woman with a rifle in her hands.

"We are lost," I barely managed to say, because the woman's patience was short. "We are looking for a place to stay. Our brothers were killed and now we are alone."

She came up to us and touched our heads with her hand, and now we will definitely not lie about our identity.

"So, you're the "Inkwellers", she said calmly, lowering her weapon. 'Ours!' the woman shouted, and the bushes began to rustle with incredible volume.

We realized that we would be accepted here.

The Cold Planet

5

This wonderful woman's name was Chayil, she is the mother of a dark-blooded girl, and this place is the only place where no one goes. Well, almost no one. They live in the neighboring house, so she was one of the first to hear that something was wrong and immediately ran to find out. Her daughter, Lilia, is ten years old, and they have been living here for five of those years. Chayil is an ordinary person with warm blood, so she has a regular job and works in the city. No one knows about her cold daughter, "it's the best option for her safety," she says. She kindly treated us to tea with sweets, which we hadn't seen or tasted for several years. For Vilas, it was a special gift that made him almost cry. It was the kind of milk cookies our mom always brought to him, when she was alive. Chayil didn't ask much about us; she preferred talking, so she couldn't resist telling us about her friends from the village.

"In fact, most of the people living here are illegal immigrants. However, there are indigenous people who remained despite the radiation. One of them is Grandma Hershem. She used to be an elementary school teacher but is now retired. This kind woman is happy to teach my Lily and several other dark-blooded children.

"As I understand it, she is not like us, but like you," I said quietly, as if asking a question but also answering it.

"She is like all of us," Chayil hugged her daughter, "she is human. And it doesn't matter that you have darker blood than I do, we are all the same people. I understand this, you understand this, and I wish the stupid government would understand. Since you are our future, children like you are proof that humanity will not die out! And they, those scoundrels, are killing our planet even more by doing so. By creating useless stuff that pollutes the air and fills the planet with radiation. This is wrong, but when those fools realize it, it will be too late. Nature, God or some other higher power above us has given humanity a second chance! A chance for a new life, but there are always idiots who spoil everything," said Chayil.

She said it in one breath

t was very clear that she had accumulated a lot of thoughts over the years, which she was eager to share. And the main thing is that I completely agreed with her. She had a profound understanding of life, and she believed that all of this could have been avoided.

Vilas was eager to play with his new friend. I could partly see envy in his eyes, although he had learned to hide it well. I realized that his envy of Lilia was based on two differences between them: 1) she went to an underground school that Grandma Hershem had set up in her house; 2) she had a mother. For a boy of twelve, who is as developed as a girl of ten, these little nuances made it a little difficult for him to fully relax. But I believe this will pass; it has to.

They accepted us as their own. Chayil arranged for the school for Vilas, who had been dying to go there all his life. He knew how to write and read, but his skills were weak and there was no opportunity to develop them. Only occasionally did we get our hands on pieces of newspapers and old comics. And that fantastic book about the history of Ukraine that Markus stole from a bookstore.

It was incredible that a man, Iron Pickerson, also our neighbor, lent his hands and tools to clean up our yard. He cut down all the overgrown trees with his own hands, except for the fruit trees. He cleared the area of stumps, and everyone helped him with this. Then he laid bricks in the places where there were not enough in the house. He made the floor of the house by sawing boards from the same felled trees; he bricked the stove, which was the most reliable, and laid a small fireplace next to it, bringing the chimney through the stove.

Chayil and Grandma Hershem gave us some pillows and sheets, and Lily gave us a handmade carpet. Other neighbors brought a sofa and a folding chair that smelled like rats, but it was better than sleeping on the floor. We were very grateful to these wonderful people for their help. However, I didn't really understand why we needed all those warm sheets and the stove, but such attention from people warmed my heart. I wish Rad and Markus could have been there with us.

Every evening, Chayil's family had a certain ritual that brought together almost half the village. It was a TV news session that only Chayil had, because only her house had a signal from one TV channel, which showed the news of the day at 8 p.m. And so, in order to keep up to date, all the people would flock to watch the news. We were curious too, because we were waiting, waiting for something good (like everyone else, probably), but in vain. As usual, the news was not good. The TV was broadcasting only negative news and the anchor said the same thing as every day.

"Everyone knows this news!" shouted an old man in big glasses, waving his cane.

It was time for some new news. It was the news of the week, where the Minister of Law Enforcement and the General spoke openly, with

The Cold Planet

the Minister of the Armed Forces of the World standing by his side like a faithful dog (although it should have been the other way around). A thin, unpleasant man in a white coat spoke into the microphone on the podium. He was the scientist who started the hunt. He said that the experiment was a success! People were immediately alert. Everyone thought in their own way. Personally, I thought that finally this oppression would come to an end. I hoped that they had found a vaccine against the cold and that we would live normally. But as it turned out, the experiment was to make superhumans. Specifically, the aim was to tame the unique individuals with dark blood, transforming them into the perfect soldiers. A perfect soldier in terms of an obedient super-soldier made of superhuman beings who are not afraid of the cold. They move quickly and almost invisibly, a kind of mutant. But why do they need it? There shouldn't be any wars, precisely because there are no separate states where all people are different, there is a single planet where the main enemy is superhumans like us. So, what is the essence of this army? The answer was total control over the entire human race.

"Does this guy think he's God?" the old man shouted, while everyone just silently held back their tears.

This could have been the end of the story; it was already deplorable. However, what I saw brought me to tears. They showed the army up close and among the men and women I saw Rad and Marcus. At that moment, I could not be stopped without additional force, because it was real hysteria. They were there on that screen, alive, but not alive at the same time. Glassy eyes, like a puppet's, a blank look. They were wearing gray overalls, like all the caught sheep of the government. I knew that it was them, their faces, their bodies, but they were not the guys I was carefree with that night. No soul, just a shell.

I was screaming in a voice that was not my own, and I vaguely remember what happened next.

The Cold Planet
6

When I woke up in the morning, Vilas was sitting next to me, holding my hand. He was sleeping on the floor with his head on my bed. From the interior, I realized that I was in Lilia's room. Everything was so gentle, girlish. I woke Vilas up with my uncontrollable movements.

"You're awake. How do you feel?" he asked in a sleepy but caring voice.

"But somehow it is not clear. My heart is beating fast."

"Don't hold back, Viola. Don't! You're making it worse for yourself," he said like a real adult. I threw myself into his arms.

"They were there... so empty... their eyes... their eyes..."

It was hard to string words together. I wanted to say so many things, but only tears broke out. It was difficult to hold back the flow, as though something was squeezing me tightly from the inside. Like some kind of spasm or cramp. It was really painful! I covered my face with my palms.

"Vilas, did you see them?" I finally managed to ask.

"I saw," he looked down.

"They've been caught, Vilas, they've been caught!" I shook his collar, as though I were demanding money.. My hands were shaking like an old woman's.

"But they're alive. They weren't killed!" Vilas tried to speak in a joyful voice, but his eyebrows were furrowed in a less than happy way.

Chayil was standing in the doorway! I saw her, but she didn't dare to come in. For several minutes she held a tray with cups of fragrant tea, which I could smell. Her hands were shaking as much as mine, because she understood what Vilas and I were going through. They all did. But when our voices died down a bit, Chayil decided to come in.

"Drink some tea. It will help to put your thoughts in order and calm your soul."

"Thank you," Vilas said and handed me a small cup.

I picked it up with trembling hands, pouring hot boiling water over my fingers, but I didn't care about the pain the boiling water brought. My thoughts were elsewhere. At that moment, I tried to calm down a bit to set my mind to action. At least a small one, at least to force my heavy body to rise, but at the time it seemed to me a very difficult task. I stayed depressed for several days. It seemed that everything just collapsed when I saw my brothers. Many thoughts went through my head, and one of them hasn't left it to this day: "It would be better if they died than to be taken by them". And for almost a month, this thought did not leave me. I think if the guys could think, they would think the same way. After all, the only thing worse than death is being caught.

It took me a long time to think about it, and it ended when I finally realized that at such a young age I could do nothing. I am only 16 and no one will listen to a stupid little girl. At that time, age became my enemy, which I could not get rid of or change at all. That's why I started making a plan. I came up with what I believed was a brilliant idea. I decided to gather my own army and fight all those idiots who were in charge of this world. I recruited all the red villagers who worked in the city to take them here when they found dark-skinned people. Normal people don't go to this place, but we are not considered normal either. That is why my little plan began to come into effect.

During this time, Grandma Hershem's school began to grow. Within two months of this search, instead of three children, twenty-four children aged eight to fifteen started attending the school. Abandoned houses where it seemed no one would ever live again found their owners. The village began to flourish! I was proud of this work, even though there was a great risk in this case. It could have been discovered! In such a case, Iron invented hiding places underground. Although it was difficult to dig through the frozen ground, he managed to make a safe hiding place. All able-bodied men were called to work and began digging tunnels under their own homes. Grandma Roska, who had an eye disease that allowed her to see far away, was put on guard. At eighty-eight years old, she had an excellent memory, thanks to which she knew every resident by sight. And when strange or armed men appeared on the horizon, she would give a signal, namely, by making a scene with her neighbor. In this way, she would distract the people coming this way by holding them off for a few minutes with her conversation. Having a naturally incredibly high-pitched voice, she can easily pull off scenes with shouting and quarreling. She is a talented woman! I've heard her quarrel more than once and I can honestly say that it's impossible to argue with her. Of course, the security is so-so, but the main thing is that there is a storage facility. It's so strange, reminiscent of those terrible times when the Germans hid Jews in

The Cold Planet

their homes. In fact, people have always behaved so brazenly.

Finally, I went in search of new people. It's not that I wanted new experiences, I was just tired of sitting at home. At least Vilas is going to school, but I'm just sitting around, so I decided to leave. Maybe I'll find some part-time work. Moreover, people say that there are fewer guards on the streets, which seems to me like a breakthrough. Summer was coming to an end and it was gradually getting colder outside, but fortunately for me, this cold didn't scare me. The city center was too crowded and so I decided not to go there. walked around the neighborhood, looking at the residential complexes with graphic paintings decorating their walls. Modern graffiti was a form of art that was punishable by a large fine, and graffiti artists were hired specifically to fill these gray buildings with color. No new buildings were built, but the old ones were beautifully decorated. I managed to find a part-time job there. During my walk, I came across a process of spray painting the walls. A local craftsman, Pavlus Lopermal, was working. He is an artist for the soul, as he does not take money for his masterpieces. He has a full-time job at a company, but painting is his hobby. I have never had the opportunity to meet him in person, as I have only heard some of his biography from Rad.

I did not dare to come closer because I did not want to interfere with his work. But I did not go unnoticed.

"Hey, down there!" he shouted, standing on the lift.

I did not pay attention to these shouts because I could not understand that he was addressing me.

"Hey, black braid in a hood, I'm talking to you." His brief description of me fit the bill.

"Are you, to me?" I pointed at myself with my index finger.

"Yes! I'm sorry for being so rude, but could you please hand me a brown spray can?"

I went to the bag that was lying on the floor below and rummaged around inside and found the paint I needed.

"I found it!" I shouted, lifting the can up to the top to show it off.

"Throw it!"

The spray can was thrown several times. First, too high, which almost hit the artist himself, then too low, and then I barely caught him to prevent him from falling to the ground. However, the next time was lucky, as it hit the graphic artist directly in the hands.

"Thanks."

Having finished the last line, Pavlus Lopermal went downstairs. He took off his gloves and began to thank me for my help. I could only be ashamed, because this man turned out to be incredibly handsome. His hair was disheveled and his eyes were shining with an incredible smile at the work he had done. At that moment, I decided that I had never met a more handsome man in my life.

"I don't know how to thank you. I wouldn't have dared to climb this structure again, because I'm very afraid of heights!" he whispered in my ear.

"Really?" I asked in surprise.

"It will be our secret, okay?" he smiled his uneven smile at me. "I'm Pavlus!" the man held out his hand to me, but I reacted quickly.

"I'm not dating!" I replied flirtatiously, or so I thought.

"What a pity! Because I wouldn't mind painting your portrait, cutie." His words were honey to my ears.

"You can go to jail for saying that," I smiled a naive smile.

The Cold Planet

"Come on!" he started to pack up his waste. "Well, if you don't want to get to know each other, then maybe you're looking for a job? I know it's a bit of a struggle right now, but I have a simple offer."

"I didn't like sexual slavery, so suggest something else," I tried to joke, but I always failed at it, but I made him smile.

"No, of course it's not an exciting profession like that, but it pays well. And even minors can get a job," he looked at me with a stunned look.

He handed me a business card with phone number and address.

"This is a business card from a friend of mine. He is recruiting people to hand out flyers in the city center, and I think you can try it. Think of this part-time job as a small payment for your help. It's my job to give it to you, and yours to use it or not." He smiled again. I never thought I'd like a crooked smile.

"Thank you for the offer. Of course, I wasn't looking for a job, but it's worth taking advantage of such a gift of fate. By the way, I'm Viola!" I decided to introduce myself.

"I am very pleased to meet you. I hope this is not our last meeting."

After that, we parted ways and continued on our own paths. I headed to the center, where I managed to get a phone in one of the coffee shops and called this mysterious number. It was surprising that these places were working perfectly in such a terrible time. I wish I didn't have to be afraid to visit them.

That's how I managed to get the job. The interesting thing was that the name "Pavlus" was the key in this conversation, and it was easy to negotiate with him. Upon arriving at the designated address, I received a pack of paper leaflets and was then sent into the city to distribute them. The man looked tense, as if he knew I was one of them. Although there was nothing to give me away. I was even wearing gloves and completely wrapped in warm clothes, which made me uncomfortable and restricted my movement.

Armed with confidence and a backpack full of flyers, I went to the most crowded place. I was glad to see the absence of guards. I could breathe easier without them. However, my surprise was indescribable when I saw Rad there. My heart was racing looking at him. He stood there in a strange costume that looked like a knight's armor, but definitely not made of heavy metal, as it was in the

Middle Ages. In his hands, he held a stick, which he used to point at each passerby; as I understood it, this stick was indicating the 'inkwellers". I think they are looking for us here. Now it became clear why people said that there were fewer guards, because they were replaced by robots. However, these were not automated metal killing machines, they were new generation people who had been rehabilitated. Rad, as I saw him, was different, even though his face remained the same.

It was scary to look at him, because my feelings were raging inside and divided into two parts. One part wanted to run up and hug Rad, and the other part made me stand and work without attracting attention. However, when I finished handing out flyers, I decided to take a chance and walk past Rad. He looked at me, but his expression did not change. But when I walked by and was insanely close, he grabbed me, but did not look at me. His eyes were riveted on the crowd, showing no intention of drifting in my direction. He was looking straight ahead, holding that stick in his left hand and holding me with his right. That's when I realized that something was about to happen.

My heart began to race, and I did my best to pretend that everything was normal. But what he did next knocked me out, as he began to trace Morse code on my palm with his fingers. I didn't know it well, Vilas knew it better. But I could understand that Rad was giving me a signal. And the only thing I could make out was the word "go". It became clear to me that Rad, my Rad, was still here. He was worried even when he was restrained.

Letting go of his hand, I rushed home as fast as I could, surprisingly forgetting about the promised payment from the leaflet distribution. My mind was full of memories of today's meeting with Rad and I was very worried about him. I hope they are at least feeding him something tasty.

At home, we were able to partially analyze Rad's message with Vilas, as I am good at memorizing such things. I can call myself a tactile person. I was able to partially recreate Rad's touches and this is what we got: "What the hell are you doing here? Hurry up and go home before someone catches you."

"In general, it sounds like Rad," Vilas said, smiling warmly. "But didn't he say anything else?"

"I don't remember more. And even then, I'm not sure it was exactly like that," I racked my brain.

"Well, it's okay. I'll go tomorrow!" Vilas cheerfully volunteered.

It was hard to resist, so pushed him on the shoulder.

"Are you stupid? It's very dangerous!" I was angry, furrowing my brows.

"I know, but let's be honest anyway. I'm smarter than you!" my brother rubbed his shoulder, squeezing his left eye.

"What do you mean?" I didn't like what he said, but it was true. If I had been able to understand what Rad had said to me at that moment, perhaps we would be thinking about other things now.

The Cold Planet
7

No matter how much I resisted or persuaded Vilas to stay home, it was all in vain. That cunning fox had escaped in the morning while I was sleeping. He got out through the window because the door was propped up, making it impossible to open from the inside. I deliberately locked him in the room, because I had a hunch about his plan. Still, Vilas was right; he was smarter, because I had no idea he could get out through the window. I didn't even think about it, it was a terrible defeat. I could only wait or do something stupid and follow him. So, I did something stupid and followed hi! I didn't have a clear route, but I had a rough direction.

I didn't find him in the center where the high-rise buildings are, but I saw Marcus standing where Rad used to be. I was afraid that the Morse code prank had somehow led to my brother being replaced. But my sadness dissipated when I saw Rad on the other side of the cold bridge. He was trying not to look at me again, and I was trying not to attract attention. My clothes didn't stand out much, so to seem more believable, I tried to shiver like most of the people passing by.

Later, I saw Vilas sneaking up behind Rad. He tapped his arm with his fingers, signaling his arrival. Rad didn't react, but it was clear they had started to make contact. It was so noticeable that it seemed like everyone on the planet could see it. Perhaps I was a bit overwhelmed because I was very worried about my boys at the time. I was afraid that Vilas would be caught and I would be left alone. Even now, I don't know how to act correctly, and without the clever Vilas, I'll lose my spirit.

Their communication didn't last long. Rad was forced to leave his seat and move to another one. In general, I do not understand why those evil people use people like us. Is it possible that only a certain number of people on the planet realize that we could all exist peacefully?

What do they want to achieve with this? Vilas brought me the answers, and after talking to Rad, he began to understand a lot. At home, he and I began to discuss this difficult topic for us.

"What, what did Rad say to you?" I waited impatiently for an answer.

"Oh," Vilas sighed, "I don't know where to start. He gave me so much information at such a frantic pace that I even think he was rehearsing before I arrived. It was like he was tapping his fingers to get the information out to me faster."

The Cold Planet

"So, what was it about?" I was either curious or excited, but I wanted to know the information immediately.

"First, he yelled at me for coming, and then he praised me for my courage. And just so you know, it happened in a split second. It's strange, but it's not," Vilas smiled, nervously running his fingers through his leaky gloves.

"Go on!" I hurried him.

It made my heart beat wildly.

"Uh-huh. Then..." Vilas paused for a moment, his brow furrowing, and then he appeared to freeze, lost in deep thought. "Then he started talking about how they were caught. He said Marcus had been shot with a sleeping dart that night and that Rad couldn't get him away quickly because he lacked the strength. That's why they were caught, because Rad was not ready to leave Markus alone. He said he would have done it for everyone. So, they were caught and put in a car, and there they knocked Rad out with a sleeping dart. When they arrived at their destination, they were unloaded from the car as if they were animals to a slaughterhouse. Rad saw many other vans with children, girls, and pregnant women getting out of them. And the main thing is that the pregnant women were the "Inkwellers". This was a new generation that scientists were eager to study." Vilas drank some water; it was a little difficult for him to speak. "Their arms and legs were in some kind of shackles that blocked the force. They weren't heavy, but they had a feature that prevented them from moving freely and made it impossible to even jump up easily. This is a breakthrough in technology. Really incredible."

"The scoundrels," I said, "They are doing everything to make us weak."

I stared at the white wall without blinking. Anger pierced me to the core.

"Then he said that the area where this crazy building is located was hidden by some kind of power barrier, because it is simply impossible to hide such a large building. It is sixty stories high. It's hard to believe, but that's what Rad said," Vilas said. – "He added that those who were brought were divided into groups. Women in one column, children in another, and strong and tall men in yet another. There are crazy inventions that the authorities are hiding from humanity by making with impractical waste, such as household appliances and inoperable weapons. But this is all just a cover, as most of the technologies are produced underground. They carry out experiments, and only when everything works perfectly do they present it to the world. There are space inventions there that are hard to believe are real. Rad mentioned a couple of names, but I couldn't make them out because it was the first time I heard them. He even described his suit to me, because I asked him "why aren't you looking at me?". It turns out that they had some kind of chip implanted in their brains, in the part responsible for vision, which allows them to see everything they see. And if Rad looked at me, then the whole group sitting in the room watching everything from the screens would be looking at me."

"It's scary!"

It was hard to realize the scale of this. Are there really hundreds of people in such laboratories as guinea pigs?

"Yes! And the main thing is that people are not even aware of the existence of such technologies. They think it's just a replacement for guards, like an improved version. Better trained people to hunt down the dangerous us. But certainly not dark-blooded people with artificial chips to track and trace a new generation of people."

"And what do we do with all this? How do we save them?" I thought I hadn't voiced these questions, but they came out of me in a voice.

"No way," Vilas shrugged, saying it quite calmly.

"What?" I asked disappointedly, as I was expecting a different answer.

"I asked Rad the same thing and he said "no way". They have cameras all over the world, and even beyond it, there are satellites flying around watching the Sun and other planets. Scientists are looking for a new planet to move to, but so far, they have been unsuccessful."

"How does Rad know all this?" I could not understand.

"They were trained. Before they became these living robots, their team underwent special training and they were told everything, but on a certain condition. In addition to the vision chip, they were implanted with a bunch of different chips that, if they disobey, simply heat up to hellish temperatures and burn the carrier from the inside."

"What a terrible death. They are just scoundrels!" I was furious, although I really wanted to cry from such helplessness.

"I agree with you, sis. But Rad warned us not to wander around too much, because they know about this village where we are staying. They also know that there are a lot of "Inkwellers" here, and so they can visit at any time. Rad warned us to be ready for a meeting. He even suggested that they could send him and Marcus here and they would be unable to do anything, as they would be acting on the protocol laid down by the chips."

"We will not survive their offensive. Only a miracle can help us."

8

Walking the streets was becoming more and more frightening and dangerous. The streets were partially empty, and the "Inkwellers" units were growing. There were more and more recruits in the army. And our meager plan to save the village seemed insanely primitive to us, since we could not cope with the weapons. Moreover, our army consisted mostly of old people and children. Even the village pitchforks would not help us, no matter how sharp their limbs were.

Sharing the information with Chayil did not make her feel better. On the contrary, she became more nervous for her daughter and the other children. Staying here was no longer a safe haven. The realization that the authorities knew everything about everyone made it worse.

"Sometimes it's better to live without knowing!" Chayil once said.

If she had any lust for life before, she seemed to have lost it. All of her neighbors were grieving with her. Although she was a warm-blooded person, she was loved and respected by everyone.

Despite this, life in the village was gaining momentum. People began to put their farms in order, or rather, they started from scratch. They plowed up the frozen ground on which they built large greenhouses, where they managed to get temperatures above 15 degrees. This was just enough to grow some food and grass for feeding the animals. As for the birds, they mostly kept ducks, since they were the least affected by the harsh weather. Of course, they had more fat than meat, but it was still a very necessary product. Sheep became more common, but their wool was only partially sheared, as their thick coats were the only protection these wonderful creatures had against the cold. Unfortunately, other animals could not survive the cold. The farmers tried to build warm buildings, but it was difficult to survive in winter, when the temperature reached minus 48. It wasn't that people or animals were afraid of the cold weather; it was the unexpectedness that caught them off guard. The weather forecast for recent periods has been extremely inaccurate. Because they broadcast one thing, but in reality, everything changes and turns out to be something else.

That is why the animals did not survive. When they are outside at minus 15, and in a few minutes a storm comes and the weather deteriorates to minus 50 in a matter of seconds, it is impossible to react in time. The same thing happened to people. Humans could not stand this sharp cold and simply froze to death in the open air.

However, a great achievement was that the oceans and seas did not freeze. But I think this is a temporary phenomenon. Because of the cold temperature, fish that lived on the deep bottom began to swim up and people were able to catch them. Fish was considered a delicacy, extremely rare in the markets, and incredibly expensive. The same was true for the meat of any animal. All food products began to rise in price, but this happened all the time, so people were no longer surprised. It seemed that humanity was just waiting. Waiting for its historical end, namely the moment when the star goes out completely. But it has been scientifically proven that if the Sun goes out, it won't be forever. Instead, it will enter a kind of hibernation, which could last for an unpredictable amount of time. A long time ago I read in one of the magazines that after the Sun exhausts its hydrogen supply, there will be a gravitational contraction of its core, which will lead to a temporary decrease in activity. However, later it will start burning helium, which will give a new burst of activity. This phase, however, will not last forever. When this stage is over, the The Sun will eventually enter the white dwarf stage, becoming a residual but hot remnant of its core that will gradually cool over billions of years.

The Cold Planet

Thus, the Sun will not "go out" in the literal sense, but will move into a new state, symbolizing the end of its active phase as a star. This process is natural for stars like the Sun and is called stellar evolution.

However, this information was denied when it started to get cold. Later, new articles appeared that began to really scare people. But with the emergence of a new kind of people, everything changed completely.

It has been said that if the Sun were to go out instantly, all the people on the planet would simply freeze, and this would not affect their lives in any way, as everything would essentially freeze in time. When the Sun embraces us again with its warm rays, we will thaw out without even realizing it.

This is exactly the kind of noodling that the leaders of our world have been putting in our ears. I personally do not believe in this. There are a lot of scientific facts that prove it. They, in turn, used very abstruse words to ensure that ordinary people would not understand and would not fear death. If the Sun were to go out instantly, the temperature on Earth would begin to drop rapidly. In a few days, the surface of the Earth would turn into an icy desert, and people deprived of sunlight and heat would not be able to survive. The average temperature of the Earth would drop to -73°C in about a week, and most life on the planet would perish. It's hard to say whether we would survive, but all warm-blooded creatures certainly would not.

In terms of time, if we think logically, the Sun is located at a distance of approximately 150 million kilometers from the Earth, and the light from it reaches us in 8 minutes. Therefore, people on Earth will only notice the fading of the Sun after this time. However, there would be no "freezing in time".

So, unfortunately, no "defrosting" could take place after the sun returned, because if it was suddenly turned back on, people would not be able to survive it.

Although it is hard to find a person who is not afraid of death, because everyone is afraid of it. Even those people who say that life means nothing to them will save it at the first danger.

But we waited. We waited for changes and prepared for the worst. Studying the history of mankind, it seems to me that in every era, people have expected the worst and hoped for the best. This dichotomous view of life is deeply rooted in human culture. Many historical texts, works of fiction, and even scientific articles show how people, realizing the difficulties of their time, have always strived for a better future, even if it seemed impossible.

The death of the planet did not frighten us as much as the possible attack of the military from the new nation to which we belonged. It's hard to fight against ordinary people, but it's even harder to fight against your own. I'm afraid to imagine how Marcus and Rad would feel if they had to stop Vilas's and my hearts from beating with their own hands. I think that after that, they will make the chip inside them explode to end their own existence.

9

The winter was cold, as the forecast that had been promised came true. The sun was dying! It was getting colder and colder every day. People felt it all the time, but we did not. I was frightened to see how Chayil was suffering, wrapped in all the blankets in the house, even though they provided no warmth at all. Her temperature was falling along with her vital signs. We were preparing for the worst.

I could feel the frosty air. It burned my lungs like the fire of a hand. Even I felt it, but it was pleasant and somehow free. But for all the other humans, it was getting harder to breathe. We tried to make a fire, but it did not burn and did not warm. Only small flames were playing on the remains of the wood, as if mocking those who wanted to warm themselves in such a fierce cold.

It seemed that the level of oxygen on the planet was falling with the temperature. But there was something magical about it. Watching everything around you crystallize, turning sharp and snow-white, is simply unforgettable.

"It's so bbbbeautifuuuul," Chayil said as she watched the glass on the window become covered in frosty patterns. "It rrreminds meee of childhooooodddd," she said through the chatter of her own teeth and smiled with frozen lips.

These words were the last to leave her mouth, accompanied by warm steam, like a spirit departing from a body. Although, perhaps it was, because Chayil was covered with a crust of ice. Her skin glistened, slowly developing frosty crystals that gently settled upon her like tiny gems, creating a magnificent shine on every inch. Every second in the winter silence, more and more frosty coating was on it, turning it into a real ice sculpture that seemed to merge with the winter surroundings.

On January 21, there were severe frosts, as the star was expected to begin hibernation. It seemed that no thermometer could measure such cold; they simply cracked from their inability to indicate the appropriate temperature. Chayil and most of the people in the village were covered with an ice crust at minus 63 degrees Celsius. They looked like statues. That was the last time I looked at the thermometer. There was no point in continuing, as there were no living warm-blooded people in our environment. I will not speak for the whole world. Perhaps some of the rich survived by hiding in warm bunkers, or they invented special capsules in which to hibernate. There are many options and I can only guess and fantasize. Perhaps only fantasy was all I could afford in this life. If we believe in reincarnation, who was I in the past to deserve this life now? Most likely, not a very good person, because good people are not hunted.

Sometimes I think that being warm-blooded is better than being like me. Because right now I would be freezing like everyone else, instead of watching the suffering of people I love. Watching this is much worse.

I saw tears rolling down Lilia's cheeks like hail. The strange thing was that they froze almost as soon as they touched her cheek. She was in Vilas's arms, an unprotected child like my brother. And there are many of them.

The animals were frozen in dead pictures. They still seemed to be in motion. Everything around was slowly turning a crystalline white, covered with a thin crust of ice that reflected the pale light, making it seem as though nature was crystallizing. Every gust of wind carried with it the frigid breath of winter, and the ice steadily gained strength. The heavy branches of the trees, bent beneath the weight of ice, cracked silently as each new layer added frozen beauty to this shimmering world, where time seemed to stand still and eternal winter reigned. There was more and more ice, and fewer living things around. Even my fingers looked darker than usual, although this was probably because the sun was no longer shining and darkness was engulfing everything around me. The power plants were freezing and breaking down, causing lights and lanterns to go out everywhere. However, this did not affect us in any way, because I realized one thing that I could see even in the cold darkness.

At the same time, all people were preparing to die. I didn't know for sure whether all of humanity would die or just a part of it. Because in this cruel world, the strongest survive, although this is not about this situation. Right now, nothing depended on human strength. If everyone freezes, then everyone and everything will inevitably freeze. Nature will cease to flourish, and all water and wildlife will freeze. Everything would die in just one moment.

The Cold Planet

The world was silent. Everything stopped! All the people were sent home, no one worked because they were spending their last days with their families. I was hoping that at least now this war that the government had invented for itself would stop. Maybe I was not the only one, but no one thought about it anymore.

I really wanted Rad and Marcus to be with us in these last days, but they were not. They got lost and separated from our pack, they were not released, but kept in cages. It was unbelievably scary. Sadness tore my soul apart. It's even worse than receiving a diagnosis of an incurable disease; I believe that's similar to how a sick person feels when they know they are facing imminent death. Now the whole planet felt like that.

...

It happened at night, from January twenty-first to twenty-second.

People froze along with the planet... But who are we, the "Inkwellers" or HomoSuperior, if we are still alive?...

Ruslana Okhrimenko

Manufactured by Amazon.ca
Bolton, ON